The Animated
MENORAH

Travels on a Space Dreidel

written by Ephraim Sidon
created in clay by Rony Oren

SCOPUS FILMS

From the series
The Animated HOLYDAYS

Series Editor: Uri Shin'ar

D1406723

Published by Scopus Films (London) Ltd.
P.O.Box 565, London N6 5YS
P.O.Box 21377, Woodhaven, New York 11421

Graphic design: Tamar Zelenietz

Photography: Avi Ganor
Art direction: Rony Oren & Avi Ganor
Photographed in Frame By Frame Studios
Educational consultant: Udi Lion
Text consultant: Prof. Seymour Simckes
Print production: Ehud Oren & David Melchior
Printed by G.D.I. and covers by Tal Press

Project producers: Uri Shin'ar & Jonathan Lubell
Made in Israel by Jerusalem Productions Ltd.,
23 Abarbanel Street, Jerusalem 92477, Israel

© Copyright 1986 Scopus Films (London) Ltd. All rights reserved.
ISBN 965–328–000–7

No part of this publication may be reproduced, stored in a retrieval system or
transmitted in any form or by any means, electronic, mechanical, photocopy-
ing, recording or otherwise, without the prior permission of
Scopus Films (London) Ltd.

FIRST CANDLE

Call me Danny.

I'm nine and my sister Judy is ten and a half. There's also Mom, Dad, Grandpa Sam and Grandma Rebecca. That's my family in a nutshell. Actually we're pretty famous, ever since our appearance on 'The Animated Haggadah'. Tons of times kids stop me on the street and ask, "Hey, were you on 'The Animated Haggadah'?" I answer, "No, I was on The Hannukah Show," and laugh.

Why do I pick Hannukah? Because it's the holiday I look forward to most, with all the candles, fun and games, latkes and presents. Okay, I get gifts on other holidays. But I really work for them. Take Pesach. I have to find the afikoman. That hidden piece of matzah! It means crawling under the table, checking behind Grandpa's back, rolling up the carpet. Sure, I always find it, but until I hold it in my hands I'm a nervous wreck! As for Purim, before I win anything I have to qualify as 'the most beautiful' or 'the funniest' costume.

But on Hannukah everyone wins. So if you want to talk presents and holidays, Hannukah is no sweat and a real knockout. And when you add in the dreidel and the fact that I can strike a match without Grandma saying, "Don't burn the house down," then Hannukah scores even more points.

Best of all are the stories. About miracles, hand-to-hand combat, victories. In other words, if you were to ask me, "Danny, what holiday would you take along with you to a desert island?" I'd answer without thinking twice, "Hannukah!"

Boy am I lucky it's already Hannukah. I have a dreidel in one hand (Grandpa's gift) and a latke in the other (thanks Mom), and it's time to light the first candle. Judy and I flipped a coin and I won. Grandpa says the blessing, I light and we all sing. Then Grandpa begins a story about an ancient Greek king called Antiochus Epiphanes.

"Long ago, he ruled over many lands including Israel. He wanted everybody to worship idols, like he did. Naturally, the Jewish people refused, and therefore, Antiochus declared the Jewish religion illegal. No more Torah study, Bar Mitzvahs, circumcision, Temple worship. Nothing. Anyone caught being Jewish was tortured to death.

"One of the saddest stories is that of Hannah and her seven sons. They were caught and brought before Antiochus. They all refused to bow down to the idol. One after the other, all seven sons were executed. Hannah then jumped from a window to her death. But she was glad that none of her children had betrayed their nation or their tradition."

"Awful, awful, awful," sighed my sister Judy. "What heroes. They all died?"

"Yes," said Grandpa, "rather than worship an idol."

"How many were they?" asked Judy again.

"Seven," repeated Grandpa.

"Eight," insisted Dad. "Eight including Hannah, and eight means it's time for bed!"

So Judy and I went to our room, got ready and turned out the lights. We stared at the menorah on the window-sill with its two glowing candles (the first and the Shamash) and the melting wax.

Judy spoke first, "Ya know, when I look at the first candle, I can almost make out a big nose and moustache. What do you see?"

"Yeah! Plus a crooked chin," I exclaimed. "From this angle, I can see a human face!"

"A creepy face," whispered Judy.

"I bet that's what Antiochus looked like," I said. "You know, I've never been as angry at anybody as I am at that lousy king. I'd like to punch his face inside out so nobody would ever recognize him again. But the trouble is he's not around anymore," I complained. "Anyway, it's not fair — all the miracles happened so long ago, that there's nothing left for us."

"Who says there are no more miracles?" asked Judy.

And suddenly an idea flashed in my head. I stood on my bed, shut my eyes tight and shouted, "Let there be — A MIRACLE!"

Those were my exact words. Abracadabra and hocus pocus weren't good enough for a holiday. I yelled again, but before I could finish my sentence, the dreidel Grandpa gave us began to get wider and taller (you can ask Judy if you don't believe me). Both of us sank into our beds, speechless, while the dreidel kept growing and growing till it reached the size of a regular spaceship.

Buzz buzz, whirr whirr, click click.... Rocket noises filled the air and blue sparks flashed everywhere. On the side of the dreidel where you'd expect to see the Hebrew letter "NUN", which stands for miracle, a door swung open and out dropped a staircase.

I peeked at Judy. Her mouth was open as wide as the dreidel door. She says that's how I looked too — I can believe it! Terrified but unable to stop ourselves, we tiptoed toward the dreidel and clambered aboard.

3

We saw hundreds of computers and dazzling lights, like in some outer space film! At the center of the spaceship was the biggest computer I ever saw. And the screen flashed: "Insert floppy disk into drive."

"Yipes," I said, "where can we get a floppy disk?"

My sister was cool. She took from her pajama pocket a latke she kept there, so she wouldn't have to run to the refrigerator in the middle of the night, and inserted it into the computer. The computer ate it up, and from that moment on, I decided to feed it only latkes!

All of a sudden the door closed and the dreidel lifted clear off the bedroom floor. We shot out through the window, higher and higher and higher still until the bright city lights below disappeared completely. Judy and I were now totally alone in a black sky full of stars. We decided to name our spaceship "Star Dreidel".

"Where are we headed?" asked Judy.

Immediately the main computer monitor displayed: "Palace Antiochus". That made me happy because I really wanted to settle the score with that louse.

After ten supersonic moments of space travel, we spotted lights. Slowly, Star Dreidel touched down. The door opened, and Judy and I found ourselves in a gigantic chamber. Luckily Star Dreidel landed right behind an enormous pillar, so nobody noticed us. Smack in the center was a huge throne, and on it sat a king with a crown, surrounded by fierce soldiers.

"Look," said Judy, "look at that face!"

Wow, his face was just like the one we'd seen in the melting candle in our room.

"It's Antiochus," I said. "We've come to the stinker's castle!"

And while I was figuring out how to stuff his face with my fist, a squad of soldiers dragged in a bunch of kids about our age. Those poor kids were shaking like leaves.

"Your Majesty," said the commander, "we caught these brats studying Torah in a village near Jerusalem."

"Torah?" said Antiochus, biting his nails, stomping his feet and crossing his eyes. "Torah?" And he faced the children, thundering, "You Hebrew brats have a lot of nerve! The penalty for breaking my law is death. But I'll offer you a way out. See this idol here? Just bow down and you're home free. If not..." and he traced one finger across his throat. "I'll give you five minutes to decide," he said leaving the room.

Those kids did nothing but shiver. We had to do something fast, or they would be history! Judy and I scrambled out into the open and beckoned them to follow us. You should have seen how our funny clothes and the huge dreidel scared them — but anything is better than death! Okay, we practically had to drag them into the ship, but in the end they boarded quickly, realizing that it was their only escape. I zoomed round the chamber a few times, trying to attract the soldiers toward us. They charged at the ship, hitting us with everything they had. Who were they kidding? Bows and arrows against a spaceship! Then they dropped to the floor as I passed once over their heads, and we sped off into the black yonder of outer space.

"Where to?" asked the computer.

I almost answered, "Home," but then remembered our crowd of kids. So Judy and I shouted in triumph, "To their village."

Star Dreidel hung a U-turn. In five minutes we were in sight of their village, but there were swarms of Greek soldiers there. So the kids directed us to land outside the village near a cave, which they said was their regular hideout. We went inside and checked it out. Not bad!

Just before we lifted off, two of the kids presented us with their sandals. Wow, genuine old-fashioned sandals, with those extra long straps, like they wore in the Bible!

On the way back to our room, we were real lucky — our window was still open. So we dove into our beds. Then Star Dreidel slowly shrunk to its normal size. We hid the sandals under our beds and fell asleep. That is, Judy did. But I got up and checked the dreidel once more. If I hadn't been a passenger, I'd never believe such a trip....

SECOND CANDLE

Call me — skip it, I already told you! Well, you can bet your Hannukah gelt that Judy and I could hardly wait for the second night of Hannukah.

We lit candles, sang, spun the dreidel (it pretended not to be a spaceship) and ate latkes. Then we prepared ourselves for the continuation of the story, this time told by Grandma.

She explained that Antiochus' plan almost worked, but finally the Jews came out fighting. Their leader was Mattityahu, an old Jewish priest from the Hasmonean family of the village named Modi'in.

Caves became not only their new homes but also their military headquarters. There Mattityahu and his sons, Yochanan, Simon, Judah, Elazar and Jonathan, organized thousands of freedom-fighters to face the Greeks on the field of battle some day.

"How many?" I asked.

"Thousands and thousands," repeated Grandma.

"No, eight," said Dad, blinking an eye. "Because it's bedtime."

No problem, we went to bed. Our menorah flickered on the window-sill.

"I think I see something in the candle," said Judy.

"What? Like a beard?" I asked.

"Could it be Mattityahu?" whispered Judy. "We'd better check on those guys." She opened the window and hollered the magical formula: "Let there be — A MIRACLE!"

Our dreidel grew and grew just like before. And we were off again, two dreidelnauts hurtling through space.

We found Mattityahu's sons in the cave where we had said goodbye last night — or was it? Boy, were they surprised to see us! Then we heard soldiers outside. We all flattened against the wall.

"C'mon out with your hands up," roared a soldier, "you unseemly Semites!" We kept still. "If you don't know what's good for you, you'll soon find out what's bad for you," laughed another soldier. They started piling up branches at the mouth of the cave. "Have your last smoke," joked the soldier, "but smoking may be hazardous to your health!" And he torched the pile.

Before we knew it we could hardly breathe or see. We coughed like crazy. We almost passed out. For a moment I wanted to surrender — but only for a moment. Because suddenly the back wall began to open and a secret passageway was revealed! A little candle appeared out of nowhere, held by the spitting image of that wax face.

"Come," beckoned the voice from the blackness, "follow me."
We sure did. Not that we had much choice! The tunnel was so dark and narrow, we had to crawl. Once we had all made it through, the tunnel was sealed again, making a perfect fit, so nobody could guess where we had gone. We could hear the soldiers shouting on the other side of the wall because they had lost us.

Then we began moving. When the ceiling of the tunnel was high we walked, when it was low we crawled again. It took fifteen minutes but finally we were outside — right in the middle of Modi'in!

"Keep moving," said Mattityahu. We followed him to the village square. There we saw a platform and on it stood a white goat, a Greek idol and a Jew with his knife raised high ready to make a sacrifice.
"Now watch this carefully," shouted a soldier to the crowd. "You're next, every one of you. Learn your lesson. No more Torah study, just idol worship." Then he blew his trumpet and the Jew lifted his knife even higher, ready to plunge it into the animal at his feet.
"Traitor!" cried Mattityahu as he struck the man. A second later the man was dead, Mattityahu's knife in his heart.

Everybody froze like a statue, except Mattityahu's sons. The five of them jumped the soldiers. With the help of some villagers, they stripped them of their weapons and took them all captive!
"Congratulations on your brief victory," said the Greek commander sarcastically. "For now you may drink and be merry, but tomorrow you will all die. Because tomorrow comes the counter-attack!"

Mattityahu knew the commander was right — there'd soon be a price to pay. "All those on the Lord's side," called Mattityahu, "follow me!" And everybody did — I mean the whole village.
"To the mountains!" he commanded.

Judy and I were about to join them when we realized we had to be home before Mom waked us. So we went in a different direction, but we couldn't find the cave or Star Dreidel.

"What now?" I said, trying not to sound too terrified, but sounding pretty scared all the same.

"One second," said Judy. Then she hollered our formula for miracles. It worked! Star Dreidel suddenly spun in front of us. As we dreidelnauts boarded, I snatched two Greek helmets lying on the ground, and we were on our way.

I knew our window would be open. Back in bed, through sleepy eyes, I watched the dreidel shrink again to its regular size.

Next morning we were awakened by Mom holding the sandals and helmets. Judy explained that they were props for our school play. (I can always count on Judy.) Then Mom said, "One more thing. I found your window open again. Which one of you left it open last night?"

"Maybe you forgot to shut it," I said.

"No way," said Mom, "I remember shutting it last night. So why is it open now?"

"I opened it," said Judy, "to let out the candle smoke."

What did I tell you? For an older sister, Judy really is okay!

THIRD CANDLE

If waiting for the second night was like waiting for class to end, then waiting for the third was a billion times worse. But it was worth it. Candles, supper, games, songs, jokes — then story time. It was Mom's turn now.

It goes without saying, naturally, that none of the adults suspected that the tiny dreidel Judy and I were spinning non-stop was actually a perfect spaceship. C'mon, would any of them ever believe us if we told them of our launching into outer space? But come to think of it, if I heard my own story, I'd never believe it. Whoever heard of anyone travelling through space and time in a dreidel programmed by a latke! If only they knew what a story we dreidelnauts could tell.

Anyway, Judy and I listened to Mom tell the tale we'd all been waiting for — The Maccabees! And what a tale — of courage against incredible odds, of fighting throughout the land, of the underdogs versus the superpower.

Mom explained how the Maccabees got their name. It comes from a sentence recited at the time of another miracle — the parting of the Red Sea. Each letter stands for a Hebrew word, which together make up the phrase: "There's nobody like the Lord."

She continued, "Judah the Maccabee, their commander-in-chief, outsmarted five world famous Greek generals and then marched on Jerusalem."

I didn't believe my ears. Five generals! That's the real stuff! Just to be sure, I asked Mom again.

"Were there really five of them?" I inquired.

"Five," said Mom.

"Eight," said Dad. "To bed!"

Off we went. As usual, our menorah was shining on the window-sill. The third candle was all twisted by now. Again we tried to make out a figure.

"Now that's anybody's guess," said Judy. "Doesn't look human to me."

"Could it be an elephant?" I questioned. The more I looked, the more I was convinced.

"Give me a break," said Judy, "where do elephants come into Hannukah? Were we Jews forced to eat elephant chops?"

"Maybe the Greeks worshipped elephants," I tried. "Maybe it was one of their idols."

"We'll soon find out," said Judy. And we both yelled out the magical "Let there be — A MIRACLE!"

And once again Star Dreidel did its thing, transforming into a spaceship before you could tell a pink elephant joke. We inserted a latke into the computer and lifted off. We had no idea where the dreidel would take us this time. I figured we were going to the zoo, but soon we were coasting over a chain of low hills.

When we de-dreideled, we found ourselves on a real live battlefield. On one side were the Maccabees, and on the other the whole Greek army. But where were the elephants?

Suddenly this enormous thing stood up.... Wow! An elephant the size of a tank! On its back sat dozens of Greek officers. And stacked behind it for miles were thousands of infantry, looking like a traffic jam.

I've seen elephants before at zoos. They look like they're always having fun, splashing themselves with water or stuffing their faces with hay. But when they stampede, they're worse than tanks on hooves. Try stopping a tank with your bare hands! Absolutely no fun at all — especially when it goes berserk like that honcho of an elephant at the head of the pack, leading the whole Greek army and crushing anything Jewish that stands in its way.

The situation looked bad. Judy and I argued about what to do. I said we should re-dreidel and land the spaceship smack on top of the elephant. Judy said, "No way."

Suddenly one of the Jewish freedom-fighters, a young guy with a short beard, broke ranks, ran up to the elephant and looked him in the eye. The elephant stared back at him and began to lurch forward.

"Run, Elazar! Run!" shouted his friends. "It'll crush you." But Elazar didn't budge. He just faked that animal out and slipped below its belly. WHAM, went his long spear into its hide! The elephant tottered and dropped, squashing the generals and Elazar too.

Judy and I exchanged glances and both of our eyes froze in fear. Everyone stopped in their tracks, partly out of fright and partly out of astonishment at Elazar's courage. Nobody moved.

Judah was the first to snap out of it. He saw a golden opportunity and rallied his men against the startled Greeks. Javelins raised, they attacked as one. Without an elephant to protect them now, the Greek army began to fall like flies. Thousands were taken prisoner, all except their commander and a few hundred of his officers, who escaped.

Judah wanted to capture them also. He was sure that they'd be back again and better

organized. But it was like looking for a needle in a haystack. If only Judah could find them before they regroup.

I don't like to boast, but it was a lucky thing we were there. Zooming around in our space dreidel, we were able to search the countryside. We checked out every canyon, valley and cave, until we finally pinpointed their whereabouts.

I voted for immediate arrest, but Judy exclaimed, "Two of us against a hundred?"

"We're worth more than a hundred of them," I answered.

"Right," she admitted, "but maybe they forgot their arithmetic, and it's not worth risking it." So we returned to headquarters.

"General," I said (standing straight as an arrow), "we have found the enemy."

So Judah and his men followed us as we slowly led the way in Star Dreidel. Even so, they couldn't keep up with us, and we reached the hideout first. We put flares around the place. And when Judah and the fighters showed up, they soon took care of the remaining rabble and its cowardly commander.

"Thanks," Judah said to us.

"Don't mention it," said Judy. "Just doing our duty." But to me she whispered, "It's late, let's get cracking."

Which we did, after Judah handed us a dagger and a bow for our efforts.

We came home exhausted and proud, but depressed at Elazar's death. It's not every day I see a hero fall.

"We might have won this time," Judy told me, "but you know, even Judah got killed in the end."

"But what do you mean? What happened after we took Jerusalem?" I asked. "Does it have anything to do with why we celebrate Hannukah for eight days?"

"Tomorrow is another day," said Judy. "Maybe Star Dreidel will take us directly to Jerusalem."

But I couldn't sleep without knowing what had happened in Jerusalem. I had to know right away. So when she was asleep, I stood on my bed and whispered, "Let there be a miracle!" Nothing happened. It seemed our dreidel was designed for only one flight a night.

But I had another idea. I tiptoed to my father's study and picked out the book Mom had used for her story. I read it by myself. It was just as I had guessed:

Why do we celebrate Hannukah? Because the Greeks ruined our Temple, tampering with every can of oil. When the kingdom and Temple worship were restored by the Jews and the Hasmoneans cleaned out the Temple, all they could find was one container of oil to

keep its eternal light going. The oil was just enough for one day. But it lasted eight whole days!

I copied out the story to show Judy in the morning.

"Can you figure it out?" I asked.

"What's so difficult?" said Judy. "That's what Hannukah is all about, the miracle of light, one candle lasting eight days. Didn't you know that dummy?"

"Of course," I said, "just testing!"

FOURTH CANDLE

It's me Danny, as if you didn't already know.

Guess what? Tonight again we had candles, latkes, songs, games and the story. But it wasn't the usual because Grandpa pulled a fast one. He told us about Marranos.

"What? You've never heard of them?" I teased Judy.

"Big shot," shouted my sister, "as if you ever heard of them!"

Actually I thought it was Spanish for ice cream, but the word really means swine — the name the Spaniards gave to their kosher neighbours five hundred years ago.

Things were bad for the Jews then, like Antiochus all over again. Jews were forbidden to celebrate holidays, study Torah or keep any of their customs. Worse, they were forced to convert to Christianity! So they faked all the Christian stuff in public and at church. But at home, where the Christians couldn't see them, they were just as Jewish as ever.

The Church had its own secret intelligence outfit called the Inquisition. Their job was to find any fake converts (you know catch them in the act).

They were a real mean bunch. I pity anybody who got caught in their dirty hands. They'd burn you alive at the stake.

But many Jews took their chances anyway, despite the danger. They celebrated every holiday, especially Pesach and Hannukah. You'd be amazed to see them lighting candles and making a seder in cellars and behind secret walls. And I'm talking about thousands of people, maybe even....

"Eight," said Dad.

"More, more," said Grandpa.

"Eight," insisted Dad, and we understood why. So off we went.

The four candles of our menorah still glowed on the window-sill.

"Look," said Judy. So I looked. This time the fourth candle seemed to resemble a sinister shape I couldn't recognize — like a crooked figure with a hood and cape....

And so we called out, "Let there be — A MIRACLE!"

Up, up and away we went, faster than ever before. I was sure we were heading for Jerusalem, for a tour of the Temple itself, otherwise why the rush. But when we landed in a sombre town, I got the shivers.

"Creepy place," I said to Judy. "Is this Jerusalem? It looks more like something out of the Middle Ages."

"That's exactly what it is," said Judy. "It's Madrid in medieval times."

We de-dreideled, sensing that Star Dreidel had some purpose in dropping us off here.

"Look," said Judy. And again I looked.

Passing by was a bunch of monks, accompanied by some tough guys carrying spears. Believe me, they were no attraction for sight-seers. We trailed them until they suddenly halted.

"Over there!" said the monk at the head of the file, pointing to something far off in the distance — a thin crack of light. "Tonight is Hannukah for Jews and that is the light of a menorah. That must be a Jewish house over there. Let's catch 'em red-handed!"

"They'll soon be hot-footed too," joked a second monk.

Everybody laughed except us. This was a job for the dreidelnauts. How could we save those Marranos?

"I got it," I told Judy. "We can beat them to that house with Star Dreidel. You warn the Marranos, and I'll take care of those Inquisitors."

Zoom, we were there. Judy de-dreideled and knocked at the front door. The light immediately extinguished. The door opened and Judy disappeared inside.

I swung around in another direction, planning to mislead the Inquisitors. I hovered behind a tree and turned on the parking lights making a new target for the Inquisitors — the only one they had now. They turned around and picked up their pace. I let them walk another mile, then killed the lights, scooted off to a different spot and redirected them again. When I could see the whites of their eyes I killed the lights once more. Actually, I did it four times, once for each of the four candles. So then I doubly confused them. I stepped out of Star Dreidel with a burning candle and really drove them crazy.

Finally they gave up.

I zoomed back to those Marranos. "It's safe to light your candles again," I said in one breath. The whole family hugged us. There were four of them too — mother, father and two kids our age. They each lit a candle and sang. Then, since Judy always carried an extra floppy latke on her, we shared it with the family. I thought by some miracle it would stretch to the size of a large pizza, and we could all have seconds. No such luck. But it was the tastiest first I have ever eaten in my life.

We would have been willing to sleep over, if we didn't have to be in our own beds for Mom to cover us in the middle of the night. Otherwise we'd have to explain to her tomorrow why we spent the night in Spain.

So we headed home, after accepting some awesome gifts — a neck chain for me and a bracelet for Judy. Believe me, they wouldn't let us say no.

One last thing. When we were back in our room, Judy started to hum a melody we picked up in Spain from the Marranos. Suddenly Mom stuck her head in the room.

Puzzled, she asked, "What's all the noise?"

"Nothing," murmured Judy. "I was singing in my sleep."

"At this hour?" said Mom.

"I was dreaming about you, Mom," said Judy.

What a brain that girl has!

FIFTH CANDLE

You expect me to tell you that we sang, ate, played and lit candles. So I will. Come the fifth night, we sang, ate, played and lit candles. Dad claimed we weren't the only ones doing it. He said that Hannukah was a holiday for anybody, anytime, because the menorah shines as a sign of freedom for people who are persecuted anywhere.

But Judy loves to ask questions, so she asked, "What about Americans? Can the War of Independence be connected with the battle of the Maccabees?"

"Yes," Dad replied, "in fact, the spirit of 1776 was like the spirit of Hannukah!"

But it made no sense to me. How did Hannukah help America against the British? I thought about it and thought about it, and finally I asked him.

Dad checked his watch and said if it weren't so late, he would explain to me how Hannukah helped and so on, but since it was late, well maybe tomorrow. Sound familiar? Parents... they're all the same!

We headed to our room, where the five burning eyes of the candles were waiting for us. Actually the fifth light looked like more than an eye. To me it looked like a man, a very dignified but very sad man, and definitely in need of a little Hannukah cheer.

So I jumped on my bed and said as clear as a bell, "Let there be — A MIRACLE!"

Star Dreidel reactivated, and we were on our way — even if we didn't know which way. The stars streamed by as we catapulted into outer space.

We finally landed in a dark valley. The monitor displayed: "Valley Forge, 1777". That didn't help me, I still had no clue of where we were. But not Judy. On a game show, her category would be famous people and places. All I saw was a valley with night soldiers slumped against their weapons. And it was so bitter cold, I was sure Judy and I would come home frozen as dessert. But worst of all was the look on everybody's face. They couldn't be any more depressed and still be alive. Nobody whistled in the dark, nobody made a fire in the cold, nobody joked about anything. I thought I'd catch it too — that look of a loser.

Cut! Freeze frame! Hold everything! Suddenly we noticed a faint light flickering at the end of the camp. Judy and I went to investigate. You'll never guess what we found! Believe it or not, there was a soldier sitting in front of a genuine menorah — all five candles (plus the Shamash) burning bright.

To me that was the coolest, even neater than riding in Star Dreidel or meeting Antiochus — seeing Hannukah candles quietly burning in such a depressing place really was a miracle. And the soldier didn't even know we were there.

After a while, Judy tapped him on the shoulder. Turning, he asked, "What are you children doing here?"

"What's a menorah doing here?" I questioned.

"That?" smiled the soldier. "My father gave it to me years ago, back in Poland, with his blessings. He told me it would brighten any path I took in life. So I take it with me everywhere I go, even to this battlefield. I am here fighting for freedom in America. George Washington needs me to help establish a land of the free and a home for the brave."

I knew what he meant. I'd fight for freedom too.

The three of us didn't even realize that by now others had begun to gather around that menorah. And as they watched the flames flicker, their lips curled into smiles. Somebody was humming too.

Then there was sudden silence, as the soldiers parted to let some officer make his way through the crowd. I'll never forget the look on that face. He was a general for sure. For a moment, I was scared he'd eat the face off that soldier for lighting a fire in a blackout. But no.

"Soldier, what do you have there?" asked the figure in the night, coming closer to the shining menorah. And I saw who it was — the man in our candle. It was George Washington himself!

The Jewish soldier told the general why we celebrate Hannukah. You know, the stuff about the underdog, courage in the face of incredible odds, taking on a superpower, etc. Judy and I even added a couple of details ourselves.

"Thank you," said George Washington gently, "you have indeed lifted my spirits. For like the Maccabees, we are outnumbered and outgunned, but like them I believe that we shall overcome." And, turning to us, he added, "As for you children, you must leave camp at once. Tomorrow a fierce battle will rage on these grounds — one that will determine the future and freedom of America and her people."

You see, even if we wanted to, we couldn't hang around until tomorrow. So we lifted off in Star Dreidel.

"What next?" I asked.

The monitor stayed blank for a few seconds, as if it were thinking.

"Are you taking us home?" I asked, really impatient and tired by now.

"Wait and see," replied the monitor.

So I waited and I saw. We touched ground opposite a small cottage. In the window was

the same menorah that lit up the camp in Valley Forge a year before (actually three minutes ago). We went in. It was our Jewish soldier! He recognized us immediately and gave us bear hugs.

"You again!" he said, "I'm glad to see you, children. Happy Hannukah 1778!"

Then the door swung open and there stood George Washington. Ask Judy, ask the soldier, ask George Washington himself. He wouldn't lie.

Washington placed one hand on the soldier's shoulder. "Your menorah, which now sits on the window-sill, together with the story you told about the Maccabees, made all the difference in the world a year ago. You transformed my grief into joy, my depression into courage. I felt that your freedom-fighters of old were with me then and that I could not fail. Allow me to present you now with this memento."

He pinned a gold medallion on the soldier's chest, and then embraced him. I copped a quick look at the medallion — it showed a menorah with one candle on it. The inscription read, "Light makes right, George Washington."

On the tip of my tongue were the questions, "How about us? Didn't we help?"

George Washington must have read my mind, because he bent over, kissed Judy and me and pinned a medallion on each of us.

You can bet that the window in our room was open. Judy makes no mistakes when it comes to windows. As for the medallions, they joined our collection under the bed, so that one day we could show any non-believers the necessary exhibits!

SIXTH CANDLE

Guess who? Right. Danny.

Today my father's brother (that makes him my uncle) arrived with his wife Miriam. Boy are we lucky. We are really crazy about them and they give great Hannukah gifts. Grandpa honored Uncle Reuben with the lighting of the candles.

Then Uncle Reuben (he's a captain in the navy!) told us the real story of the Moroccan rescue operation thirty years ago, when he himself brought boatloads of Jews to Israel.

He began, "We'd dock at night in some little port in Morocco. Hundreds of Jews would be waiting for us there in the dark, because months before our agents had spread the word of our expected time of arrival. And we'd load them up and take them all with us back to Israel."

Reuben even showed us a photo of himself in uniform standing on the deck of his ship. You could even make out the insignia on his cap. It was the rank of captain. I oughta know. Reuben gave me a captain's cap for keeps once.

"How many immigrants did you bring to Israel?" asked Judy.

"Eight," said Dad.

"Are you kidding?" said Aunt Miriam. "He brought thousands!"

"Eight," repeated Dad. "Bedtime! That's an order."

"Aye, aye, sir!" we chorused.

"Lately," added Dad, "the kids give me no back talk about bedtime. They actually run to their room."

I almost burst out laughing.

At the window sparkled our menorah with its six tongues of light. We gazed at the sixth candle looking for some clue. We almost jumped when we saw that the sixth candle was curled in a circle like a steering wheel. And we yelled, "Let there be — A MIRACLE!"

All that Star Dreidel needed was a latke. Anchors away! Being the two expert dreidelnauts that we were, we buckled up as the spaceship, with a full belly, hung low over the sea. Sure enough we landed on the deck of a ship.

We went straight to the captain's quarters. If you're expecting to see Reuben again, you won't recognize him. He was so young now, with a full head of hair and no belly!

"You look just like the photo in the album," said Judy.

But Reuben had no time for a family reunion, he had an emergency on his hands. Moroccan counter-intelligence knew at which port he would dock. Practically their whole police force would be waiting there to catch everybody — Reuben, his ship and all the refugees.

Now what? He couldn't just leave those Jews stranded. But he couldn't risk certain capture.

"Let's try another port," suggested an officer. "There's a fishing village nearby. We could anchor offshore, the police won't even think of checking there."

"Your idea has two problems," said Reuben, like a true captain.
"First, the Jews of that village aren't expecting us. And there's no way we can inform them today of our arrival. They won't have time to sell their houses or their businesses. How many of them can leave on a moment's notice? Second, if nobody's waiting for us, how are we going to locate anybody? Go from house to house looking for Jews?"

Suddenly it hit me. "Hey," I said, and everybody looked at me. "Isn't this the sixth night of Hannukah?"

"What if it is?" asked Reuben.

"If it is," I said, "won't they be lighting candles? Where there's a menorah, there's a Jewish family."

I could see they were amazed. I was amazed myself. Aren't you?

"Good idea," said each officer, one after the other. Then they swung the boat around toward that little village.

The pier was deserted when we anchored around midnight. But sure enough, we could see lights here and there in the village in the distance. Jewish homes! Judy and I guarded the ship, while all the sailors went searching for Jews, following the lights. They knocked on each door, introduced themselves as sailors from Israel and asked if anybody wanted a free ride to the Holy Land.

A long time passed, and Judy and I were getting really worried. We did not see anyone coming. When we were near desperation, we finally saw a couple with a baby approaching the ship. They were followed by another couple and then more and more. They just kept on coming. It was truly a miracle considering nobody expected us. They'd all just packed up quickly and left. They didn't even say goodbye to their friends. They had no time to sell their homes and possessions. That's how much they wanted freedom and Israel!

The whole operation lasted just two hours. Not a single Jew remained in that Moroccan village. Only the candles still burning in the windows were proof that Jews once lived there.

The voyage would be four days long, so Judy and I wished them all well, and shook everybody's hands, from captain and crew to each new immigrant. Actually, they all wanted to shake my hand, even Judy slapped me five, because it was my idea. (I'm not saying I'm a genius or anything.)

We all got the same gift, a Moroccan galabia, which is a long-sleeved robe with a sash. Some dictionaries call it a kaftan. (Maybe I am a genius.)

Star Dreidel took us home. Ask me if the window was open. Of course, it was. Another job well done!

SEVENTH CANDLE

You know what's wrong with Hannukah? It lasts only eight days. And already tomorrow it's over. That's not fair!

But the seventh day was great. We sang in harmony and spun the dreidel till our fingers hurt. Did I mention already that I'm the expert at spinning it upside down? After lighting all seven candles, we gathered around Dad to hear his story.

It was about Jews in the Soviet Union who want to come to Israel and the government won't let them. They're called "refuseniks" because they are refused permission to leave. In fact, they are often sent to jail just because they request to leave.

"How many refuseniks are there in Russia?" I asked.

"Hundreds and thousands," said Dad.

"Exactly eight," said Mom, pointing at the clock on the wall.

We dashed off to our room, as Grandma said, "What's happened to those children? It used to be such a fight to get them into bed, now it's their favorite activity!"

"Maybe they have exciting dreams," said Dad.

Judy and I laughed our heads off and got into bed. We checked out the candles, and sure enough we could make out an image. The seventh candle looked like it was wearing a fur hat and thick winter overcoat. Who could it be now?

It was Judy's turn to stand on the bed and call out three times, "Let there be — A MIRACLE!"

Star Dreidel was ready for action. I logged in, then Judy inserted a latke and we began to travel through time and space. As usual, I had no idea where we were headed.

We landed in a snow covered city. It had to be Moscow because of the Kremlin towers. (I didn't need Judy for that one!) Immediately, we spotted a menorah in a window and approached the house. We peered in.

A girl our age was standing looking at the flames and crying. When she saw us outside shivering she nearly fainted, but she managed to open the door and let us in. She stammered, "Wh...where...where did you come from?"

I introduced myself as Danny and told her that we came from a distant country. Judy introduced herself and told her that we are Jewish like herself.

The girl looked at us as if we had fallen out of the sky (which wasn't so far from the truth). We all shook hands and began to talk. Her name was Larissa, and she spoke English with a funny, broken accent.

It turns out that Larissa's father was exiled to Siberia as a refusenik. The KGB had been holding him there for over six months now. Larissa hadn't seen her father all this time. I considered her a hero. I would have been a basket case if I couldn't see my father that long.

"Would you like to see your father?" asked Judy.

The girl laughed. "How could I? He's in Siberia, behind barbed wire and under guard. If they won't even let me see his letters, why would they let me see him?"

"You have a surprise coming," I said, and we took Larissa to Star Dreidel.

Larissa couldn't believe her eyes. And I'm glad. You'd have to be crazy to believe in dreidelnauts. Still, she boarded the dreidel and Judy flew us to Siberia in two supersonic moments flat.

The camp was huge. We made a quick soft landing behind trees, so as not to attract the attention of the guards. Creeping along, we searched among the huts, looking for the tell-tale light of a menorah. And then we saw it. Inside a man was crouching over, secretly

lighting candles in a menorah made of just potatoes.

"Daddy," cried Larissa.

And they hugged and kissed each other, while Judy cried. According to Judy, I also cried, but I'm not sure about that because I never cry, or hardly ever.

Anyway, Judy and I had a real argument. She wanted to give Larissa our Star Dreidel. I was against it. Not because I didn't want to help Larissa, but because I had grown accustomed to our new way of life.

"And how are we going to get home?" I asked. I didn't expect her to have an answer to that, but she did.

Larissa would accompany us back home, and then fly off with Star Dreidel to Moscow. That way she could visit her father whenever she wanted. So, I agreed. Larissa couldn't thank us enough.

Back in our room, the three of us snacked on some latkes that Judy kept under her pillow for use as floppy disks. We handed Larissa all our extras and explained to her how they worked.

It was a soppy goodbye. Standing in the center of the room, Larissa pronounced our code words in her Russian accent, "Lyet zer be a meeracle, lyet zer be a meeracle, lyet zer...."

Star Dreidel welcomed her with open doors, and the new dreidelnaut was on her way. It circled round twice, as if to say goodbye, then disappeared...forever.

Next morning, Mom woke us and said to clean up our room. We arranged all our gifts nicely (that is, the family gifts, not the gifts from our space travel). Mom was a little angry that we lost the dreidel.

"Very nice," she said. "Grandpa buys you a dreidel and you lose it."

Should we tell her that it's flying now between Moscow and Siberia???

EIGHTH CANDLE

Judy and I weren't so sad on the last night of Hannukah. Not with all those candles and all those gifts! And I ate three times my normal capacity to keep the memory of Hannukah alive for the rest of the year. Dad said we could stay up till nine.

Grandpa told us why we celebrate Hannukah for eight days instead of eighteen (which I would have liked!).

Then I said, "Ladies and gentlemen, now it's my turn to tell a story! Once upon a time there were two children, sister and brother, who owned a magic dreidel. At night it changed into a spaceship."

"But it couldn't fly unless you inserted a latke into the computer," explained Judy.

"Naturally," I said. "And Star Dreidel took them everywhere."

"To Antiochus' castle. Where they saved a bunch of scared kids from torture..." said Judy.

"And got trapped in caves," I said, "and smoked out and Mattityahu saved us."

"Saved who?" asked Grandpa.

"Those kids," I quickly corrected myself.

"And there were elephants," said Judy. "And Elazar who got squashed by one."

"And Spain and the Inquisitors and Marranos," I said.

"And Valley Forge," said Judy, "and George Washington."

"What does George Washington have to do with Hannukah?" asked Mom.

"Don't you know that story," Dad said, "about the Jewish soldier and his menorah?"

"Oh," said Mom.

"And Morocco," I said.

"And Siberia," said Judy.

They all looked at us, then at each other.

"Where do they get their imagination?" Mom asked Dad.

"Maybe they have a fever," said Grandma.

Luckily, we got a replacement dreidel. When we were alone in our room, Judy and I tried the magic formula. We screamed our lungs out but nothing doing. So instead we counted our blessings.

46

We watched our eight candles glow, until their shapes transformed into every figure we had encountered in our journeys. First came Antiochus, the terrible king; then Mattityahu, the Hasmonean warrior priest; then the mighty elephant felled by Elazar; the Marranos of Spain; George Washington; Uncle Reuben; and finally the refusenik father. So that's seven. But the eighth candle remained just a candle.

Judy pulled out our presents from under her bed, and we wore all our gifts. Picture two kids wearing Greek helmets two thousand years old, Moroccan kaftans, gold medallions on their chests, Biblical sandals with extra long straps and in each hand a dagger or a bow.

We laughed and laughed till Mom opened our door, then we froze.

"What...what...," she mumbled in astonishment. Where did you get all those things?"

I couldn't think of anything. But Judy came to the rescue once again.

"Purim's coming," she said. "We're preparing our costumes for the contest."

"There's plenty of time before Purim," said Mom. "Now go to sleep!"

We put our pajamas back on, slipped into bed and stared at the menorah.

"Hey," I said to Judy. "It's changing. The eighth candle. It's a boy."

"You mean a girl," said Judy.

"That's me," I said.

"No, it's me," said Judy.

We compromised. We decided to wait until next year!

HOLYDAYS

An entertaining series of films, books and by-products on the Jewish festivals, aimed at today's children and their families.

From the series The Animated HOLYDAYS:

* The Animated HAGGADAH (Pesach) – book and video
* The Animated MENORAH (Hannukah) – book and Hannukit

Available Soon:

* The Animated MEGILLAH (Purim)
* The Animated ISRAEL (Israeli Independence Day)
* The Animated NEW YEAR (Book and Calendar)

For additional information contact the publisher.

The Animated MENORAH

HANNUKIT®– A gift pack of eight exciting presents for Hannukah based on The Animated MENORAH. The kit provides an entertaining series of activities and games which complement each night's ceremony of lighting the menorah, singing Hannukah songs and reading a story from the book.

The HANNUKIT is a combination of educational and fun material with a variety of items designed for all ages.

We are grateful to the Gesher Foundation
for their contribution to this project.